Liz Gavin

Her Discipline

Her Discipline
Copyright 2016 by Liz Gavin

Published by Elessar Books

Liz Gavin

Her Discipline

CHAPTER 1

I need to hold my orgasm off just a bit longer. Master's grunts tell me his almost there. As if reading my mind, his hand connects hard with my ass cheek.

"That's a good girl. God you're tight," he fists his left hand in my hair and pulls it until he can claim my mouth in a deep kiss. His right fingers stretch my nipple and he explodes deep inside me hitting all the right places and making me quiver. I know he feels my flesh trembling around his shaft as it unloads but I don't say a word. Mister knows my needs.

He pulls my sweaty body against his warm chest as he straightens up. We're still kneeling on the huge bed; his dick has softened but remains nestled inside me. Master cups my big breasts and fondles them as his hot tongue penetrates my ear. I can't control a soft whimper. He chuckles and the warm air against my neck seems to connect with my throbbing clitoris. I rest my head on his shoulder.

"What's the problem? Tell me pet."

"I'd like to come sir."

It takes me a few seconds to find my voice as I have been concentrating so hard on not coming before he gives his consent. I've already done that too many times to know the consequences. They aren't pretty!

"May I sir?"

His splayed hand skims slowly down my belly until he finds my sex. His slender fingers play with the still wet curls before he cups my throbbing flesh. His palm gets moist in a heartbeat.

"You seem ready for it pet. Don't you agree?"

Master brings his wet fingers to my mouth. I lick them, "You're a good pet."

He pinches my nipple and I gasp almost choking on my juices as I lick the last drop from his digits.

Her Discipline

"At least when you want something you are. And you want to come don't you kitten?"

"Yes sir. Please sir."

"Well I'll have to think about it. You're still on probation remember, my hungry pet?"

I moan as his shaft leaves my sex and his hands abandon my body. I feel empty and cold but I don't say a word. He is right.

"I sometimes wonder if you misbehave so often just to be punished. Is that it kitten? You like the pain that much?"

"No sir. That's not it."

"You don't like when I slap you?"

His cocked eyebrow shows me he's not happy with my answer. I'm confused. Master isn't into spanking me. Not on a regular basis anyway. I don't know what to say but I know I must say something fast. The truth is always the best choice with Master.

"I don't know what to say sir. You like slapping me?"

"Who doesn't like slapping your gorgeous ass once in a while pet?" Master laughs and I sigh in relief. He's not mad, "That doesn't mean I want to spank you all the time. I'm not into that; but you do require more discipline than other subs I've had. That's a fact."

He walks towards the door and my last hope of getting my orgasm soon vanishes.

"I won't be long."

As the door clicks shut behind him, I sit on the bed and try to calm my body. I need to get my mind off my frustration, which is particularly hard in a place built for pleasure like Club Desire. I look around and all I see are Master's sex toys and accessories.

"Not helping!"

I shut my eyes but even the softness of the silk sheet against my naked body reminds me I haven't come. Trying to get that out of my mind, I lie down on the bed and concentrate on calming down my heart beats. I think I doze off or something because the next thing I know there's hot liquid pooling down inside my sex.

"What the hell?"

I sit up with a startle to see the wet stains on the burgundy fabric of the bed sheets. My treacherous body isn't helping my case. There's no watch or clock in the dungeon. I've got no idea how long Master has been gone but it must have been a while. At least, time enough to dream the new Mistress at Club Desire was fucking me. She is gorgeous! I've seen her a couple of times. I was in a scene she commanded the other day but Master didn't want to share me that time. It was a shame. I would have liked to check for myself if her full lips were as soft as they looked. A new wave of shock irradiate from my sex through my body.

"Damn it!"

I must be going nuts. How can I not notice I've inserted a finger inside my own folds? Images of Mistress's long legs clad in tight black leather are torturing me though. Where's Master? I'm doomed but my body doesn't seem to care. It's taken over control and I've become a passenger. Against my close lids, I see Mistress. My hands close around her tiny waist before caressing her round hips and reaching for her soft ass. I squeeze her perfect butt cheeks and pull her close as I bury my face in her sex.

My own wet walls clamp around my fingers as they frantically move in and out until my body explodes when I pinch my clitoris dreaming of my teeth biting Mistress's hard nub. I moan and pant so loud I don't hear Master opening the door.

"What the fuck are you doing?"

I open my eyes but everything is unfocused. The intense orgasm still rages through my body and does funny things to my senses. I should be terrified. I should at least be mortified. I'm just too sated to feel anything other than bliss.

"I'm out for a couple of minutes! What am I going to do with you? I don't want to punish you all the time but you try my patience."

His tone and features are too plainly furious for me to mistake his meaning. I have pissed him off. Big time.

"No. Stop."

His raised hand is all I need to close my mouth again.

"Don't even try. You can beg all you want. I won't listen. Get on your knees. On the floor."

I do as I'm told without hesitation.

"I could spank you so hard right now. I won't though because I'm sure you'd enjoy it. Not giving you that satisfaction. Hands behind your back."

Cold sweat runs slowly down my spine along with shivers. I've never seen Master that angry. I've upset him with my little rebel acts many times but nothing compares to the tension in the muscles of his chest and arms as he reaches behind me to put on the handcuffs. I'm so screwed.

He walks over to where an old wooden chest stands and gets a black satin scarf from the top drawer. Panic dries out my mouth but I can't beg him for mercy. Don't want to make things worse.

"I know you hate blindfolds but guess what? I don't like my subs acting out the way you do either. All. The. Time. Enough is enough!"

His last words synchronized with the knot Master used to tie the scarf around my head. It's so tight that my head throbs. I don't dare say anything. I've broken a golden rule between a master and a sub. I know it.

"I'll come back when I feel like it and if I think you deserve it. In the meantime, think about what you've done and how you can regain my trust."

Her Discipline

The bang of the door tells me Master has left. I can only pray he calms down before he returns. I like a light spanking every now and then but I'm not into the hardcore stuff. Neither does Master but I went too far this time. More than breaking a rule, I offended him. As a sub I rely on Master for my pleasure not only because he likes giving it to me but mainly because he finds pleasure in doing so. He knows my needs and he takes care of them. He takes care of me. I don't need to worry. Plus it's liberating not having to make decisions.

CHAPTER 2

I've lost sense of time a while ago but Master hasn't come back yet. I wonder if he's returning at all. My limbs are numb but I'm still kneeling on the same spot he told me to kneel.

A quite sigh escapes my lips when I hear the door opening. It was about time Master came back! However, chilly shivers run down my spine when the unmistakable sound of high heels click on the wooden floor. *What the fuck's going on*?

I don't dare speak or move a muscle though. I remind myself Master must have entered the room too since nobody would dare come into his dungeon without him. But I'm only truly reassured when I hear his footfall. Still those high heels throw me off because Master has never shared me with a woman before. He was so mad at me when he left I think he wants me to feel uncomfortable. Little does he know that I'm enjoying the idea. My clitoris stands to attention and my skin tingles while goosebumps of anticipation raise my hair. Their footsteps halt a few yards away.

"I brought help to discipline you," Master's tone still sounds curt as he yanks the blindfold off my eyes, "You will learn self-control one way or another."

Call it wishful thinking, but I sense he's not as mad at me as before. That's not to say he's forgiven me. I'll have to work hard for that. I keep my eyes glued to the floor to show him how sorry I am for my recent actions. So when she comes to stand in front of me I can only see her pointed black leather boots. She must be short because her feet are quite small. She's certainly gorgeous because Club Desire's staff is top model material.

She uses her right foot to spread my knees apart, as far as they can go without me falling on my face or ass. While doing that, she runs her leather-clad foot along the

14

inner side of my thighs, up and down both of them. The leather material is much softer than I thought it would be as it glides over my skin. The same thighs that up to a few seconds ago were quite numb from kneeling for far too long suddenly become alive and sensitive to touch. Without warning, she rubs the top of her foot under my body, teasing my increasingly wet sex and playing with my backdoor hole. *God, she's humping me with her expensive boot.*

Moving her foot slowly between my legs, front to back then back to front again, Mistress doesn't seem in a hurry. On the contrary, it goes on for a while, and her deliberate movements stoke the fires inside me as my womb contracts then expands. She chooses this moment to tap my tightest hole with the tip of her pointed boot. She taps my clitoris next. She takes turns between my ass and sex for a couple of times. I shudder, shut my eyes tight, and hiss at the exquisite sensations that spread from my sex and ass through all my nerve endings. This punishment is getting better by the minute.

"I think you've ruined my shoe. But it was worth it. I bet I could make you come all over it if I wanted to. You're very responsive. I like that," Mistress says as she lifts her foot to my face and shows me the damage. Dark spots cover the smooth, fine leather of her boot. It's covered in moisture. My moisture. My pleasure. She brings it up to my mouth. "Lick it clean."

My hands are still tied behind me, so I can't hold her foot, which hovers in the air in front of my nose. I don't want Mistress to be uncomfortable so I do as I'm told. As fast as I can, I eagerly lick away any trace but I still don't look up at her.

She pats me on the head when I'm done, "Good girl!"

Her compliment sends as many shivers down my spine as her rubbing had just done, if not more. It's not just
16

that I've pleased Mistress, but her silky voice connects with me on a deep level. It's almost as if she's caressing me. My sex is throbbing and my clitoris is as hard as it can get in response. I try not to whimper too loud but it's impossible to conceal the sounds.

"Good! She's uncomfortable," Master's voice sounds behind me. He also seems pleased with me and my heart beats in my throat. I'm so relieved to know he's not mad.

I feel something soft running down my naked back then moving slowly up. It tickles my skin. The silken touch travels along my shoulders and down my front. Now, I can see the purple feather boa she's using to tease my senses. It's working. As she circles my nipples with its tip, my breathing gets faster, raspier, and the two brown buttons jut out. She leans down and pinches my left nipple between her index finger and her thumb. She rolls and twists it between her fingers, stretching it a bit; the pain mingles fast with the

17

pleasure slowly churning inside me. I squeeze my eyes shut again trying to think of something else. It's useless. Mistress chuckles at my reaction as she repeats her actions on my right breast. I feel her hot breath inside my ear seconds before she invades it with her tongue. She darts her wet tongue in and out of my ear in rhythm with the fingers pulling at my nipples. I arch my back and gasp for air. Sensing I can't last much longer, she steps away and I hear her whispering something to Master. I can't hear what they say.

When Mistress returns to stand in front of me, she moves the naughty boa scarf down my body until she reaches my butt and sex. She hits my front and back with it. Although the material is as soft as silk, her expert lashing produces the expected results. My sex tingles in response to her teasing. When she's satisfied at my elaborate breathing, she stops the beating and hovers over me, grabbing the ends of the soft scarf in each of her hands. As I sense her putting

18

the two ends together above my head, I wonder what she's up to. *Is she going to tie me up? I'm already handcuffed.*

Because I'm trying to show Master what a good sub I am, I don't look up but I'm dying to know what will Mistress's next move be. She starts moving the ends of the boa scarf in the air, up and down, one at time, as if I were a puppet and she were the puppeteer. Only the strings are not attached to my limbs. I am straddling them. That's when I finally get her intentions.

She's fucking me with a damn feather boa. How kinky is that? The lower part of the scarf rubs against me, caressing both my sex and rear end. It's just like her leather boot, only softer. She intensifies the movements guiding the scarf so that it hits my clitoris with each pass. My juices are getting the purple of the scarf darker and darker, each time Mistress rubs it, up and down. She moves faster and faster. It's increasingly hard to breathe or think and I fight to keep my moans down as the sensations build inside my treacherous body. But Master notices my reactions. He knows me too well.

"She's enjoying this way too much. You're supposed to punish her."

"But she's so gorgeous. I get wet just looking at her nipples turn hard and her skin grow pinkish. She's perfect! I'm so glad you've decided to share your little pet today. I've had my eyes on her for quite some time."

I can't deny I'm proud she thinks I'm beautiful. I live to please. But my sex throbs in anticipation. I've never been with a Mistress before. Sure I've had sex with other girls but I've never submitted to a woman before. I'm glad Master had this idea. But I need to be careful not to show him how happy I am or he'll find a different punishment for me. One I wouldn't enjoy as much. It wouldn't be easy since I love most anything Master does to me but I'm sure he'd find a way for me to enjoy it less. So I concentrate on calming my breathing down.

Master unties my wrists and smack my ass, "Climb on the bed you naughty thing. Kneel down on the center. Hands on the back. Turn towards the foot of the bed. Keep your eyes down."

I scurry to obey him but steal a quick glance at Mistress as I find the right spot to kneel down on the huge four-posted bed. She's a stunning redhead with an hourglass figure that was made for sinning. I want to feel her large breasts in my hands and taste her on my tongue. I feel hot liquid pooling inside my sex and run my tongue over my suddenly dry lips.

"God your pet's killing me here."

I see her hand flying to her crotch and adjusting her skin-tight leather pants. And I notice her fingers lingering and playing with her sex over the hard material. She can't touch me unless Master tells her it's fine to do so. I think he's torturing both of us. He must have sensed our connection. I lick my lips again in anticipation.

Her Discipline

"I know you want to touch her, my dear. And I'll let you do it in a little while," he tells Mistress. "First, let me show you how I like to treat this pet."

He arranges my body on the bed, spreading my knees as far apart as possible. He scatters kisses over the soft skin of my belly while running his big hands along the gentle slope of my back and over my butt, and my long, strong legs. He slaps my backside. Hard.

"Turn around pet. Bend over. Touch the mattress with your forehead but keep your hands together at your back. I don't want to tie you up again. Show Mistress your perfect butt," he commands as he slaps me one more time.

This position exposes both my rear end and my sex to their eyes. I can't see their expressions but I know my flesh must be glistening in the low light because I feel the moisture coating the top of my legs. When Mistress speaks, she confirms my suspicions, "Look at how wet she is."

"She's a little dirty pet isn't she? Let's see if I can make her squirt," Master chuckles.

He knows that's not very hard to do. He cups my butt cheeks in both his hands and squeezes them together a couple of times.

"Her ass is delicious! I love to fuck her there."

He then decides to illustrate his points, "I paddle it."

A hard wooden paddle connects with my rear end a dozen times. He showers the blows equally on both cheeks. Each time he smacks hard, he smooths my trembling flesh with his hot hands. It's a delicious torture.

"I lick it."

I feel his wet tongue moving over the burning spots the paddle had just created. He takes my breath away but I don't move.

"I bite it."

Master nibbles the innermost curve of my butt cheek, close to my crack and I see stars.

23

Her Discipline

"Would you like to help me out here?"

I feel a pair of soft, warm hands cupping my butt then spreading the cheeks apart as Master's finger runs along them. I have to clench my teeth not to jump at the sudden rush I feel inside my sex. A gush of hot liquid escapes me and coats my thighs. I hear both Mistress and Master laughing at the evidence of my excitement.

"Wow that was fast! I guess she doesn't mind the rough treatment though," Mistress's laughter is hoarse and the sound causes even more juices to squirt out of me.

"No, she doesn't."

Master's hand cups my sex and collects my honey so that he can spread the moisture over my tightest hole using it as lubrication as his finger plays at my entrance. "You can touch my pet as you like, my dear."

I immediately feel her lips on my shoulder as her hands keep spreading my ass to help Master penetrate me. He has two fingers inside my body now, stretching me. It's not painful but it's not pleasant either. My sex feels empty in contrast but my inner walls start to tremble in response to the way Mistress is licking the skin on my neck. She alternates licks and little bites and I start taking deep breaths to delay my climax.

"That's a good pet," Master slaps my butt as he pulls his fingers away from my ass. "You don't get to orgasm from this. It's your punishment. Kneel down straight again."

When I obey, he moves his hands up my front all the way from my knees to my breasts. He avoids touching my throbbing sex though. He doesn't want to satisfy me but I know my breasts are too tempting for Master. They are large and spill out of his hands when he cups them. He fondles them and plants wet kisses in the well between my mounds, breathing in my scent at the same time Mistress kisses the middle of my back. Then she moves down towards my butt, scattering open-mouth, wet kisses over it.

Her Discipline

Master ends his exploratory journey on my face. He grabs it with one hand and whispers in my ear, as he kneels on the bed beside me.

"God you're gorgeous. Your skin is glowing. I'm glad I brought a Mistress for you today. I know it should have been your punishment but I spoil you too much."

My mouth is slightly open, begging for his touch and I gasp because Mistress is kissing my back entrance, teasing me with her naughty tongue. She spreads the cheeks and invades me with her tongue where Master's fingers had just been.

Master runs a thumb over my full lips. It's a feathery touch. He inserts the tip of his thumb inside my mouth, past my teeth and slides it over my tongue. I instinctively suck it, licking his digit as I feel his shaft stir to life, nudging the flesh on my right hip. He shudders and inhales sharply then stares into my green gaze. His blue eyes are half covered by his lids.

He covers my mouth with his and plunges his tongue inside it. I twirl my own around his. He tastes, teases, consumes me. I feel lightheaded then purr and clutch at his broad shoulders for balance as Mistress grabs my hips to keep me in place. Master leaves my mouth to kiss his way down the white column of my throat, biting hard then softly, sucking and licking it.

As he returns to my mouth and resumes kissing me, Mistress leaves my ass and kneels behind me. She rubs herself over my back then reaches around me to grab my breasts. She covers them with her hands, pushing them together, pulling one nipple at a time between her fingers. She bites my neck as she stretches the tips of my nipples until I think I'll pass out from the intense pleasure these two gorgeous creature are creating but I can't surrender to.

Master reaches down between our bodies and finds my sex. He inserts the tip of his index finger in as if to gauge the temperature. He finds me at boiling point.

Her Discipline

"Cool down," he tells Mistress. "If we keep this up she'll come all over my hand. We don't want that, do we?"

"No, we don't. She has a lot to do today before we allow her to come."

I don't mind the way they talk about me, as if I'm not here. I am Master's pet and he can treat me like that. I'm also happy they've noticed I wouldn't last much longer. I breathe out a sigh of relieve.

"Why don't you sit down over there, dear?" Master suggests Mistress and points at the overstuffed armchair facing the bed. "You'll have a front row seat to the show."

The beautiful redhead accepts the invitation and sits down. She's still fully clothed while I'm completely naked and Master still has his pants on. He gets off the bed and stands at the foot, between Mistress and me.

Master turns around to face me, "Crawl on your fours and come here pet."

When I get to the foot of the bed, he grabs my head and stabs my mouth with his hard erection, over the cloth of his pants. I gasp but he gives me no time to recover, working his arousal against my damp cave and I open it to be able to breathe.

"You know what to do."

Using only my mouth, I open the fly of his pants as fast as I can. He pulls out my prize and drops the pants to his feet. He kicks them out of the way. I run my tongue along the silken shaft, caressing, stroking Master's flesh. His breathing falters and I smile at the way his cock jerks against my tongue, swelling, begging for my attention. I can smell his arousal. I am dying to swallow him whole, to feel the large mushroom head against my tongue. *It's so beautiful.*

I sigh before start kissing his hardness. I swirl my tongue around the tip of his shaft and suck the drops of moisture, the salty taste teasing my senses. I breathe in his musky scent as I open my mouth to enclose him. Master groans when my breasts rub his naked thighs as I move against him.

I'm not allowed to use my fingers around him, since this is my punishment, so he guides his shaft inside my open mouth. He tangles his hands in my black curls and clenches his jaws. The obvious effort to keep his body under control tells me how much I affect him. I close my mouth around his rod, pushing it slowly inside the wet heat of my mouth as the wicked tip of my tongue flicks across his slit. When I run my tongue along his length, bottom to top, his thighs quiver. He manages to keep his balance by digging his fingers into my hair, scraping my scalp. But he can't suppress the roar that escapes him.

I feel his ecstasy reflected in my own aching sex. My clitoris is hard and the moisture that has been pooling between my legs slowly overflows my sex and drips down my thighs. We can all smell the scent of my arousal but I'm only concerned about his satisfaction. My gratification is in knowing that I can give him so much pleasure. That's reward enough today.

I bob my head up and down, going faster as his member slides down my throat. He's so big I need to open my mouth wide and breathe through my nose to accommodate his girth. My moans come out muffled because of his shaft and I make loud slurping noises. I feel Master's balls tighten under my chin as I suck him hard. Master is so frantic he fucks my face like he would do to my sex. He shows no mercy.

"Argh!" he wails as his control slips away.

I swallow his semen when he explodes down my throat. I suck his shaft hard and lick it thoroughly. I don't want to waste a drop of his precious essence. I look up at his beautiful classic features, which are now contracted in a mask of unadulterated ecstasy. His head is thrown back, his deep blue eyes are closed to the world, and his mouth hangs open. His muscular body is still shaking. He is a vision of lustful beauty and fulfillment and I'm responsible for that. That's power and I thrive in it. I sigh deeply. As my mouth releases his softening cock, I wipe my mouth and kneel in front of him, proud of myself.

"She seems amazing." Mistress says but I don't lift my eyes to her.

"You have no idea. Why don't you get a taste and judge for yourself?"

In a second, she's on the bed beside me. She's completely naked now and I can see she's been playing with herself while she watched us. Her shaved folds are glistening. Her soft body presses against mine and her eager, hot hands touch my sex. Her slender, naughty index finger circles my entrance, searching for my clitoris. Her wet, delicious mouth teases my breasts, biting and licking my nipples.

"I'd like her to touch me too. Can she touch me?"

"You can touch your new Mistress. It will please her and me," Master is sitting on the chair now, watching us through half-closed eyes. He has put his black slacks back on but I can see they're already tenting.

I cup Mistress's breasts. They are bigger than my hands and her silken skin is hot and sensitive. She takes a deep breath as goose-bumps form over her skin. I'm sure other parts of her body are standing at attention. I rub the soft globes hard and she trembles. She closes her eyes in abandon and for a crazy moment, I forget I'm somebody else's pet. I forget where we are, and indulge in a little fantasy of my own where I can please her in any way she wants. She throws her head back as her body sways slightly under my hands.

I look at Master and search his expression for any sign of disapproval or annoyance at my behavior. I find only a smug smile playing on his lips. He signals me to go on and I obey. I'm very happy to so. I decide to give him a sex show he will dream about later. I see him open his fly, take his huge member out and hold it. It's already stiffening again.

Master had brought Mistress to help him give me a lesson. He needed to discipline me. However, I'm enjoying this too much to call it punishment. I look at Master again and his member is harder. I guess he's not upset, either. So I concentrate on the delicious sensations Mistress is arousing in me. It's hard to breathe and my heart is beating fast. My fingers are trembling a little as I keep kneading her soft breasts under my hands.

"You can look at me pet," she says softly inside my ear.

I shyly lift my gaze and feel lost when I meet her clear blue eyes. I reluctantly lean down until I feel the warmth of her breath mingling with mine. I stop, unable to decide what to do next, afraid of something I can't quite figure out.

"Why don't you kiss me? Aren't you happy with your new Mistress?"

She teases me, a sensual smile splitting her delicious mouth. She knows how much I'm enjoying her and is confident enough in her power over my body to joke about it. I hesitate a little longer, staring at her tempting lips. She frames my face in her small, soft hands, holding me in place; then seizes my mouth in a passionate kiss. Her tongue invades me without mercy or hesitation and she sucks my tongue before nibbling on my lower lip. It's full enough so that she can suck it inside her own mouth. She sighs inside my mouth.

"You are so hot."

For a long time, the only sounds that fill the room are the moans, and gasps, and wet noises we make as we deepen our kisses and explore each other's bodies. Mistress squeezes my breasts together; then, kisses them with her open mouth, licking my nipples until they are hard. She

35

suckles at them. I can't breathe for all the intense sensations so I gasp for air and she chuckles but my big breasts muffle the sound.

Then she crashes my breasts with her own large ones and uses her nipples to tease mine. It's a kinky feeling which gets to my very core. My inner walls tremble and my legs shake. Her skin is so soft and hot against mine that I arch my back to give her full access. She follows my movement with her own body and we topple over on the bed in a heap of legs and arms.

I take advantage of our new position, with Mistress on top of me, to cup her sex and tease her opening with the tip of my fingers. She squeezes her thighs shut and traps my hand between them. She moans and stretches my nipple with her teeth while the searing pain sets my sex on fire. Mistress pries my legs open with her own as her fingers find my clitoris and circle the little nub, rubbing it fast and rhythmically to make it even harder.

"Do the same to me."

I immediately follow Mistress's order and mirror her movements. When I think I can't take so much pleasure any longer, Mistress pulls her fingers away from my wet sex and I whimper.

"Don't worry, hungry pet," she laughs as she easily flips me over on the bed and I find myself face down on it.

Mistress sits on my ass and humps it with her drenched sex as she rubs her hands on my shoulders and back. It's the best massage I've ever had. She reaches around me and tweaks my nipples. I shriek and she crushes my mouth against the mattress.

"You don't have permission to do that."

I try to control myself but it's hard to even concentrate. My thoughts are as scattered as the sensations she brings to me. Mistress flips me over once more so that I face her. She's still straddling me as she leans down to kiss me and I sit up to meet her halfway. I suck at her full lower

37

lip, twirling my tongue around hers as I hold her shoulders. She bites my lip and slaps my breasts. I cry out in ecstasy and she enters my vagina with two fingers, spreading them, moving them inside me, then in and out of my wet channel. I shudder in her arms and reach around her to grab her butt cheeks and squeeze them together. I gasp and feel my climax building as my folds grips her fingers.

"You're so tight. You feel like a glove around my fingers."

Mistress utters the words inside my ear as her own breathing gets erratic. I don't want it to end so fast so I try to regain control of myself. But I'm drowning in the sea of pleasure this woman's creating around us. I moan as the sensations mount and the sexual tension coils inside me. My inner walls quiver, my juices are overflowing and my legs are weak. Mistress turns to Master when she notices my orgasm is just around the corner.

"Are you going to allow her to come for me?"

"Well she's been a very naughty, hungry pet today. I don't think she deserves it but I see you're enjoying her. I don't want to spoil that for you. So you can play with my little sex toy for a while longer. You deserve to have some fun. Would you like that, my dear?"

"Yeah I'd love that."

"Okay so be her Mistress for this little impromptu scene. Do whatever you want with her. And if she comes for you, I'll deal with it later."

I don't have time to speculate on his meaning because she lays me down again on the bed and her hands spread my thighs wide. She pushes my ankles up and folds my legs against my upper body until my feet touch my butt. I am exposed, on display for Mistress and Master. That's hot and horny. I see Master pumping his hard shaft as I feel the cool air hitting my scorching flesh. My folds are damp and glistening with my juices and the way Mistress licks her lips tells me my enlarged pink flesh is inviting her to taste it.

"Do to me exactly what I'll do to you. Got it?"

"Yes, Mistress," I promptly agree.

She moves above my body until her own dripping sex is aligned with my face, then, she lowers herself until it's inches away from my open mouth as she leans forward and stops a few inches above my sex and inhales deeply.

"Oh, my god, you're so hot!"

My inner walls are melting even before her wicked mouth covers my folds in the most intimate kiss. She digs her fingers into the soft flesh of my thighs to hold my legs in place as her pink tongue traces the outline of my folds, licking up my honey, slurping the evidence of my lust for her. The more she teases me, the more honey she has to taste. I jerk my hips up towards her mouth as my whole body ignites at the sweet invasion. I mirror her actions and bury my face in her scorching, wet folds. I wish my tongue were longer so I could go deeper. As it is, I dart it in and out of her, twirling it around it, teasing her sweet spots, circling her hard nub. Exactly like she's doing to me. I grip her thighs and I know my nails will leave marks on her silken skin but I can't control the urgency. I want her so much it hurts.

"You are driving me crazy."

Mistress speaks against my flesh and the vibrations of her soft voice echo inside me. I roll my eyes and clutch tighter to her. I grab her ass, pulling her down on my mouth. I know that if I don't cool my body down, I'll come all over her face but it's getting harder to do so by the second.

She tempts me further by pressuring her wet tongue to my clitoris following it with blows of hot breath. The heat and the pressure; the alternate cold and heat; all shoot straight to my brain and play havoc with my body. I push my hips up, grinding my sex on her face at the same time as

Her Discipline

I pull hers down to me and suck her clitoris inside my mouth with all my might.

Mistress grabs my hips, digging her nails in my butt to keep me in place. She darts her tongue in and out of me, flicking it over the tight bud of my clitoris, nibbling at the little button and rasping her teeth on it. I gasp as the sensations envelop me and breathe deeply trying to keep the waning control over my body but her scent is intoxicating. I look at Master begging for mercy.

"Sorry pet. You're hers for now. You'll climax when she allows you. You need to learn discipline. Your hungry sex has already caused you a lot of problems today. Don't tempt me."

I need to make her come if I want any release of my own. I clamp my mouth on her clitoris. She writhes and invades my core with her fingers, fucking me with them, as she also clamps her hot mouth around my clitoris and suckle me. I mirror her movements and fuck her tight channel. I'm sure I won't survive this as I double my efforts inside her wet folds. I slurp her juices as they trickle down my chin.

Sensing my control is slipping away, Mistress sits up beside me on the bed and eyes me. The cool air strikes my exposed and tender flesh. I take a deep breath and let it out as a soft moan. She leans down and kisses me. I taste myself in her tongue as she tastes herself on mine. It's a mind-blowing feeling.

We lose touch of reality as she lies down on top of me, our soft curves grind against each other, breasts rub against breasts, wet folds against wet folds. She moves her body up and down mine then straddles me again, grinding her sex on mine, riding me, pinning me to the mattress, fucking me without mercy. She doesn't need a strap-on to make me see stars. The feeling of our hard nubs rubbing against each other is enough. Our bodies are slick with sweat and juices. The friction brings new and endless waves of lust. I know that sweet oblivion is not too far. I want to get lost in her softness but I need to obey both Master and my new Mistress. I whimper under her as my whole body trembles. I don't have permission to speak unless they address me first so I can only beg her with my eyes.

"Hold on a little longer pet. I'm almost there."

Mistress closes her eyes and throws her head back. She wails in ecstasy and her body shudders on top of mine. She tumbles forward and kisses me hard and long. My mouth absorbs her hoarse cries of pleasure as my hips move up to meet her body. My self-control is hanging by a very thin thread when Mistress releases my mouth to whisper in my ear.

"Come for me, my precious!"

I obey her immediately. I buck and thrust my hips up to grind myself against her still trembling sex as my own flesh explodes. I soar as high as I can go on the waves of the climax my new Mistress gives me. I think I black-out for a second or two before I come down again and discover myself on the bed and in the arms of my Mistress. The sweet, relaxing feeling doesn't last long as she pulls away from me, sits on the bed, and gives me another of her dimpled smiles. I melt inside and regret losing her touch.

"I'm sorry pet. I wish we could go on but it's your Master's turn."

"You did great. Both of you my sweet girls."

When he speaks, I turn my head to find him kneeling at the foot of the bed. He had taken his pants off again and his glorious, huge rod is up and glistening with moisture pooling on its large purple head. My mouth waters and I lick my lips at the sight. I want so much to taste it but he ignores me and turns his attention to Mistress who's wiping her chin clean of my juices.

"Do you need help with that?"

"I sure do."

"Come here then."

Her Discipline

He grabs her head and crushes his mouth against hers, sucking at her tongue, licking the rest of my essence from her face.

"My pet tastes divine, doesn't she?"

"Hell yeah!"

"Now she'll take care of you again while I fuck her delectable rear end. You sit up against the headboard and relax. Pet, get on your fours. Face your Mistress."

I promptly obey him.

"You'll pleasure your Mistress until she comes on your tongue this time. I don't want to hear a word from you though."

Mistress lies down on the silk cushions and opens her legs wide for me. I smell her arousal and lick my lips. I'm worried though. Master's cock is so large he always hurts me a little when he enters my backdoor hole without some preparation like an ass plug or something. I hesitate to assume the position so Master swats my butt. He showers

46

me with a series of alternated, open-handed smacks that redden my skin at once. I think I'll burst into flames but I manage to stay quiet under his blows.

"Now be a good sub and do as I tell you. Don't make me repeat myself."

I lift my ass in the air, in front of him, as high as I can. My face is almost touching Mistress's sex. She's so aroused again I can smell it and feel the heat coming from her slick entrance.

"You can use your mouth and fingers to make her come. But you can't touch her above her waist. Be creative pet. She can touch you any way she wants though."

Mistress smiles at me and I hear Master opening a drawer and taking the lube to coat his rod. A few seconds later, he's splitting my cheeks apart and shoving the tube inside me.

He doesn't waste much time because his climax is not very far either. I saw him pumping his hardness all the while he watched Mistress fucking me. Before finding my tight backside hole, he enters my drenched, still vibrating flesh to coat his dick with my own juices. I shudder at the sensation of his big head circling my entrance and he slips inside my channel, almost all the way in. The slap on my clitoris comes fast as lightning after he withdraws from me.

"Be careful, my little horny pet. I told you to behave. I won't let you come if you don't."

I stop moving and stand as still as a statue.

"Concentrate on the task I gave you. Let me take care of your pleasure."

He runs his big hands up and down my back, from my shoulders to my thighs before returning to my ass. He squeezes my butt cheeks together. Then he licks them, sinks his teeth on them and blows cool air on the bite marks. My legs tremble and I have problems thinking straight.

"Do as you're told."

He spanks my ass, again and again. My breasts jiggle as my body moves back and forth under his blows and Mistress cups them. I grit my teeth and try to concentrate on my task. I lower my mouth over her smoldering hot folds. The sweet perfume of her desire invades my nostrils. I want to grab her soft breasts and grind myself against her whole body but I can't. So I lick her wet folds and circle my tongue around her hard nub as I had done just a few moments ago. I suck it inside my mouth and suckle at it as a child does at his mother's nipple. Mistress moans and arches her back, pushing her hips up and forcing my face deeper inside her sex.

She reaches for my breasts again and slaps them. Her assault combines with Master's body and the scorching pain is almost too much. I flinch and try to escape him. He holds me in place by digging his nails into my hips.

Her Discipline

"Don't do that! It'll only make the pain worse. Take your mind off of it. That's why I've told you to concentrate on your Mistress."

He is right. I relax the muscles around his cock at the same time as I use two fingers to stretch Mistress's channel and dart my tongue inside her. I twirl it around her hot, wet cave, slurping at her juices. She's so excited I almost choke on her honey.

As I feast on Mistress's sweet sex, Master impales me in one swift movement. His rod goes all the way in, up to the hilt. I feel full and it's very uncomfortable. The pain sears through my body, starting in my ass, radiating to all my muscles and focusing in my clitoris. I shriek.

Mistress holds me by the hair and silences me with her body. I go back to eating her. I pump my fingers in and out of her slick passage, in rhythm with Master's stabbing movements inside me. Each time he bangs me, slapping his front to my back, I move forward and further into her core.

Mistress moves her hips up and down too. I'm fucking her with my tongue and fingers at the same time she fucks my face.

Master moves back and forth hammering me. I know he's rushing things on because he can't last much longer. I feel his balls tightening against my ass. He slaps me hard on each cheek in time with his movements.

Mistress pushes herself up towards my mouth and gasps when I insert two fingers in her back hole, stretching it a bit. I move the fingers in her sex and in her ass at the same time, all the time suckling her clitoris. She moans and writhes.

I hear a buzzing sound seconds before Mistress shoves a rubber dildo inside my folds. My ass is so full with Master's large cock and this dildo is so huge I feel they'll split me up in two. I want to shout out but Master had told me to be quiet. She moves the fake penis in and out of me in contrast to Master's shaft in my butt. When he enters me with the real thing, she withdraws the fake one. When he leaves me empty, she fills me up.

Mistress is very close to her climax as her walls contract around my fingers and tongue. Her movements push my body back and I collide with Master. He holds me tight as he explodes inside my ass, hot jets of semen filling me with a naughty pleasure. He wails and his shouts mix with Mistress's. I'm responsible for their mind-blowing orgasms and my heart swells inside my chest. Still I haven't gotten my own release this time.

As if he can read my mind, Master hugs me from behind and sits me on his thighs, still moving his shaft inside my ass. He holds the dildo Mistress had forgotten inside me when she climaxed. He twists it, pushes it further up my sex, hitting my G-spot and whispering in my ear.

"Come for me, my pet. I love to feel you shuddering in my arms."

He doesn't need to say it twice. I let go of what little control I had left. My body relaxes in his strong, protective arms and the waves of ecstasy crash over me. I explode into millions of pieces with the strength of my release. It's the most powerful orgasm I've ever had. It seems to go on forever and I don't want it to end. Master pumps my ass a couple of times but his cock is softening. He holds me tight, supporting my weight, because my body has turned to jelly. He slips out of me and takes the dildo away from my sex. Both my holes are sore but I don't care. I'm a happy, exhausted, but satisfied woman.

"You've worked hard for your orgasm tonight pet. I'm proud of you. Don't ever defy your Master again though."

He kisses me. It's a long and deep kiss, and we tumble to the bed falling beside Mistress. When I come up for air, I turn my head over my shoulder to look at her. She smiles at me and places her hand on my cheek. Her eyes are half-closed and her face is relaxed. I wiggle my butt against her wet folds. Her sex's still quivering. She moves one leg between mine and presses her front against my back. I feel her hard nipples rub against my hot skin. Master throws his arm over both of us, holding us tight. He kisses Mistress's mouth over my shoulder and caresses her breast. We cuddle up under the silk sheets and fall asleep at the same time.

* * * *

ELESSAR BOOKS

THANK YOU for supporting indie authors.

FOR FREE EBOOKS visit our website and subscribe to the newsletter. New subscribers receive a link to a free ebook. The newsletter will also keep you up-to-date with all your favorite authors and their releases, plus a chance to get access to special offers, discounts, giveaways and fun competitions.

If you liked this story, please rate it and review it on Amazon website. We at Elessar Books take our readers' opinions very seriously because what you say will definitely influence our future releases.

* * * *

ABOUT THE AUTHOR

When Liz Gavin was in Second Grade - just a couple of years ago, really - her teacher told her mother the little girl should start a diary because she needed an outlet for her active and vivid imagination. She was a talkative child who would disrupt the class by engaging her colleagues in endless conversations. She loved telling them the stories her grandfather used to tell her.

Apparently, the teacher wasn't a big fan of those stories, and Liz's mother bought her a diary. She happily wrote on it for a couple of months. Unable to see the appeal of writing for her own enjoyment only, she gave up on it. She missed the audience her friends provided her in class. She went back to disturbing her dear teacher's class.

Since then, she has become a hungry reader. She will read anything and everything she can get her hands on - from the classics to erotica. That's how she has become a writer of erotica and romance, as well.

As a young adult, she participated in a student exchange program and lived in New Orleans for six months. She fell in love with the city and its wonderful inhabitants. NOLA will always hold a special spot in Liz Gavin's heart. Nowadays, living in Brazil, Liz's creativity has improved many times because it's such a vibrant, gorgeous and sexy country.

Welcome to her world of hot Alpha males and naughty, independent women. Add a touch of the paranormal in the presence of some wicked souls and you get the picture.

Visit her blog at lizgavin.wordpress.com for updated information and sign the newsletter for new releases.

Other books by Liz Gavin

Sexy novels

Luck of the Irish

Upside Down

Maureen

Steamy short stories & Collections

At the club

BDSM & Paranormal BOX SET

Between the Ghost and the Dom

Club Desire Collection

Craving Her

Fallen Angel – Chapter 1

Flying High

Girls have fun

Halloween at Club Desire

Halloween Collection

Halloween no Clube Desire (Portuguese Edition)

Her Discipline

Her favorite Ghost

Her Discipline

In the Lounge

Indecent Proposal

Luck of the Irish

No Clube Desire (Portuguese Edition)

Maureen's Tale (The Dark Side Series Book 1)

Maureen's Lesson (The Dark Side Series Book 2)

Maureen's Reward (The Dark Side Series Book 3)

Powerless

Sem Força (Portuguese Edition)

Take me to the Domme

Too hot to handle

If you want to contact me, please, write an email to lizgavin@elessarbooks.com.

COVER DESIGN – Created by Elessar Erotica Books by editing an image from Big Stock Photo with Adobe Photoshop CC.

36654008R00034

Made in the USA
San Bernardino, CA
28 July 2016